a Hand

AND OTHER STORIES

Griff Gets a Hand

AND OTHER STORIES

Kit Hood and Linda Schuyler
with Eve Jennings

James Lorimer & Company, Publishers
Toronto 1987

0-88862-869-2 paper   0-88862-870-6 cloth

Design: Don Fernley
Illustrations: Heather Collins
Editor: Sheila Dalton

Canadian Cataloguing in Publication Data

Hood, Kit
  Griff gets a hand and other stories

(Kids of Degrassi St.)
Based on the television series: Kids of Degrassi St.
ISBN 0-88862-870-6 (bound) ISBN 0-88862-869-2 (pbk.)

I. Schuyler, Linda.   II. Jennings, Eve.   III. Title.
IV. Series: Hood, Kit.   Kids of Degrassi St.

PS8565.062G75 1987   jC813'.54   C87-093481-3
PZ7.H663Gr 1987

A Kids of Degrassi Street Book
James Lorimer & Company, Publishers
Egerton Ryerson Memorial Building
35 Britain St.,
Toronto, Ontario M5A 1R7

To Bruce Mackey,
the grandfather of Degrassi Street
and a dear friend of the Kids.

Playing With Time Inc. acknowledges with thanks the writers whose enthusiasm and dedication helped produce the original scripts on which the Kids of Degrassi Street stories are based — Amy Jo Cooper, Michelle Dionne, Yan Moore, Sue A'Court, John Bertram.

Contents

Connie Makes a Catch

She had to admit a baseball cap looked pretty silly
with a nylon headscarf and a prom dress. "Advice,"
she told her reflection sadly. "Advice.
Everybody's got advice."

Connie Makes a Catch

The kids on Degrassi Street were making the most of the last baseball game of the spring vacation. The game was tied at six runs each and Candy Lam was up to bat. He'd already smashed two home runs over the heads of the outfielders, and his fans were rooting for another. He warmed up to yells of "C'mon Candy! Give us a homer!" and kept his eye on the pitcher. When the pitch came, he hit the ball with a powerful swing and a "crack!" you could hear in the bleachers. As he took off around the bases, the screams and hollers of the crowd went with him.

The most ardent of his admirers, though he hadn't the least idea of it, was Connie Jacobs. She thought baseball was the greatest game in the world and Candy the greatest player. But even if he couldn't have hit a ping pong ball with a pillow, she would still have worshipped him. She was standing near the back of the crowd, only half-listening as Rachel Hewitt, in her usual steady, reliable way, talked about "doing something special" to mark their last term at Degrassi Elementary School. Rachel didn't seem to care or even notice that Connie's hero had rounded second base and the fielder was slow getting to the ball.

"Run, Candy! Run!" Connie screeched, bouncing up and down, her voice drowned by the crowd.

"Celebrate, you know," persisted Rachel, "do something special, so we remember..."

Connie didn't hear a word. Back in the ball park, Candy was speeding toward home just as a fielder shot the ball to the catcher. One second before the catch was made, Candy slid into base — safe! His fans went crazy. His teammates mobbed him, slapping him on the back and giving him the high five.

Connie looked at his sleek dark hair and almond eyes and sighed. "Isn't he gorgeous?"

"Who?" asked Rachel.

"Candy, of course!" Was Rachel blind or something?

Well, if she was, she wasn't the only one. Candy too seemed blind — at least when it came to Connie. He hardly ever glanced her way and when he did she might just as well have been one more piece of baseball equipment. She wished there was some way she could make him notice her. If only she had sizzling sculptured peaks in her hair instead of looking like a carrot with bangs. A golden tan instead of freckles wouldn't hurt either.... Thank goodness her front tooth had finally grown back in, but she still didn't look like a magazine ad. She looked like what she was, a scruffy kid in jeans. She wished she were as pretty as Lisa Canard, who had Robin Griffiths following her like a hungry puppy.

Connie knew it wasn't much use asking Rachel for advice. Though Rachel was kind of pretty, in spite of being built like a lighthouse, she wasn't interested in boys, except as fellow enthusiasts for one of her worthy projects. Still, better Rachel than nobody. At least it gave Connie an excuse to talk about Candy. "I just wish there was some way to make him notice me," she said wistfully.

"Just be yourself," suggested Rachel.

Connie might have known it was useless to ask someone who'd rather have an extra history class than a date with a boy. She muttered, "Are you kidding? Who'd ever notice me?"

Just then Lisa Canard and Casey Rothfels came drifting towards them from the crowd. Rachel didn't waste any time. "Do you realize that when we go back to school tomorrow, it'll be our *last* term before junior high, and we ought to do something to commemorate it. We've been there since we were little."

Casey offered a few suggestions, like buying a plaque or giving a big party, but Lisa seemed lost in a dream.

5

"Not a party," said Rachel. "We're having a graduation dance, remember? Any ideas, Lisa?"

Lisa blinked like someone waking up and shook her head vacantly. Casey grinned. "Don't mind her, Rachel. She's got other things on her mind." She jerked her head towards a fair-haired boy among Candy's triumphant supporters. "Griff, for instance."

Lisa went pink and pushed her friend's arm. "Casey!"

Connie wished there were some reason to tease *her* about Candy.

Monday morning was the first day of a new term. Kids were heading towards school from all directions, some reluctantly, back to the grind, some cheerfully, glad to see their friends after the spring break. Martin Schlegel rode up on his bicycle feeling very conspicuous in a bright orange and yellow vest. He'd had to wear it ever since his dad, a policeman, had given first-aid to a kid who'd broken both legs in a head-on between his bicycle and a truck. Martin tried to get the vest off and out of sight as quickly as possible. Not quickly enough. Pete Riley spotted him.

"Hey, Martin! Like your vest!"

Suspecting Pete was putting him on, Martin muttered, "Give me a break. I can't help it. My dad says I can't bicycle without wearing this stupid thing." He shoved the vest into his carrier basket and put on a pair of Foster Grant sunglasses. These had been the real cool thing to wear last term, and it had taken a lot of hard work to persuade his mom to advance him the money for a pair in time for the start of school.

When Billy Martin and Chris Moore, both wearing Indian headbands, came into the schoolyard, Martin waited to be noticed. But they passed by without a glance.

Martin called, "Hey, Billy!"

Billy turned and looked at Martin, totally unimpressed.

"How come you're not wearing shades?" Martin asked.

"Shades aren't cool anymore," Billy said casually.

"They're not?"

"That was *last* term." Billy pointed to his head. "This term it's headbands, Martin."

"Oh," said Martin, deflated. He put the sunglasses into the carrier with the offensive vest.

The term wasn't getting off to a good start for Connie either. She'd tried to catch Candy's eye several times during Mrs. Gonzales's lecture about their future at Degrassi Junior High. But even when he turned in her direction, he stared quite blankly.

7

Meet the Invisible Woman, Connie thought, watching glumly as Lisa and Griff exchanged smiles across the classroom. Finally, in frustration, she stretched her leg across the aisle and nudged Candy's foot. He looked around in annoyance, met her smile with about as much interest as he'd pay to a streetcar driver and turned his attention back to Mrs. Gonzales.

After class Connie lingered behind, trying to think up some excuse to talk to Candy. But then he was joined by two of his friends, and they left, talking a blue streak about baseball. She followed slowly behind them, too unsure of her welcome to catch up. Partway up the stairs, on the landing between flights, she stopped to watch Griff drawing a caricature of one of the girls. Pete Riley was hovering around and acting very important, like a proud owner showing off his dog's tricks. Pete had a way of looking bossy even when he wasn't saying anything. The girl's smile was becoming a bit rigid. Through it she hissed, "How long's this gonna take? I got another class."

Pete polished the air with outspread hands. "Patience, Karen. You can't rush art."

Rachel, on her way upstairs, asked what was going on. Pete said, with pride, "Griff and me are in the caricature business. I'm his business manager. I can make an appointment for you, Rachel. Only twenty-five cents a picture. Pay now, pose later?"

Rachel gave him a kind but very firm refusal.

Casey and Lisa, on their way to their next class, paused for an admiring look at Griff's artwork.

Suddenly Griff's voice echoed in the tiled corridor. "Hey, Lisa!"

She hesitated, half eager, half shy.

"Want to go to a movie or something Saturday?"

She glanced under lowered lashes at a grinning Casey. "Yeah, sure," she said, turning towards Griff.

"Great!" he grinned. As he went back to his sketch, Connie heard him say to himself, "Well, all *right*!"

There must be some secret to getting boys to look that happy, thought Connie. Maybe Lisa would let her in on it. She hurried to catch up to the girls and overheard Casey as she teased, "Everyone says Griff's your boyfriend. You're a celebrity, Lisa. No one else in grade six has a boyfriend."

Lisa gave her one of those mixed-up looks which say, Yeah-I'm-smart-but-modest-with-it-so-gimme-a-break.

Connie approached the expert.

"Lisa, I need your help. You know about boys."

Lisa tried to look cool. "Er — what's your problem?"

Connie glanced around to make sure no one was listening. "Candy doesn't know I exist."

9

Lisa and Casey seemed faintly surprised.

"You *want* him to know you exist?" Obviously thoughts of Candy didn't keep Casey awake nights.

"I like him," said Connie, a bit defensively. "What should I do?"

Casey shrugged. No accounting for tastes. Candy was okay but, well, just another boy.

Lisa felt a bit out of her depth. She appealed to her friend. "What do you think, Casey?"

Casey clicked over in her mind what the heroines of Harlequin romances did to attract their heroes. Usually they didn't have to do anything much because they were either rich or beautiful. No one could call Connie either of those. She suggested as cool and casual as she could, "Make him notice you."

"Yeah, but *how*?" demanded Connie.

"I don't know," Casey answered vaguely. "Something'll come up."

"Casey's right," agreed Lisa, happy to have a lead. "Wait for your opportunity."

"Okay," said Connie, still in the dark. "You're the expert. Thanks, Lisa."

"Don't mention it," said Lisa, glad to be free of a sticky situation.

Connie didn't have to wait very long. Most kids were eating their lunches in the sunny schoolyard. Candy sat with Griff and Pete on a bench under a

10

tree. They were examining their sandwiches. Connie heard Candy's voice, loud with disgust: "Oh no! My little brother made my lunch again! Wouldn't you know, salami and banana!"

Griff and Pete made sick faces and hung their tongues out with an expressive "Yuck!"

Inspiration hit Connie like fireworks. Seizing the moment, she advanced bravely. "Did someone say salami and banana?"

Three faces studied her.

"You *like* salami and banana?" Candy asked.

"Sure," said Connie. "My favourite. Crazy about it. Want to trade?"

He raised his eyebrows, as if he thought she was crazy, and leaned forward. "What've you got?"

"Peanut butter," said Connie, giving a boring-old-peanut-butter-again sneer and mentally wishing her lunch a sad farewell.

Candy made the exchange with relief. Connie grasped the salami and banana sandwich and took a huge and decisive bite. It was quite as awful as she'd expected, but she munched courageously, smacking her lips. Candy watched her briefly, shrugged, and turned away. Connie's jaws slowed. She moved off behind the tree, swallowed her mouthful of revolting sandwich and held the rest at arm's length. She could hear the boys laughing and was sure they were joking about her.

She went over to where Lisa and Casey were sitting. Casey was eating a peanut butter sandwich. Connie looked at it longingly. "Want to trade?"

"Are you kidding?" said Casey. "I *love* peanut butter."

"So do I," said Connie.

"So how's it going with Candy?" asked Lisa politely. Connie looked down at the half-eaten sandwich. "I don't think I chose the right opportunity."

Casey told her to keep working on it. Lisa echoed the advice. Connie sighed. As long as they didn't mean the sandwich. Stealthily she dropped it in a trash can. She looked back to where Candy was still enjoying her lunch. Oh well, you win some, you lose some. Or in this case you lose some, you lose some.

Griff looked up and smiled, not at her of course, at Lisa. Lisa wiggled her fingers in response. Then she turned to Casey. "Do you think I should wear something special on Saturday?" she asked. They launched into a deep discussion.

Connie, listening, wished she were Lisa Canard. If Griff were Candy, of course.

She wouldn't have been so envious of Lisa if she could have been in the Canard dining room that evening. Storm clouds hovered over the supper table. Lisa had just got through telling her father and her stepmother, Gayle, about Griff's invitation to the movie, and her father had come down strong.

12

"No! Definitely not!"

Lisa hadn't expected more than a few probing questions about who, when and where. This looked like trouble. "Please?" she said, trying again.

Gayle said, in her let's-be-reasonable voice, "You're too young to be going out alone with boys, Lisa."

"Lots of girls in my class go out alone with boys," retorted Lisa.

"Oh?" said Gayle, looking unconvinced. "Which ones?"

Lisa backed off. "Well, some do."

Her father was still acting heavy. "You're not 'some girls'. You're my daughter."

So that makes me special, thought Lisa, like royalty or something?

Gayle could feel the tension mounting. "Why don't you just invite the boy here?" she suggested peaceably.

Big deal. Boys had come around to play since Lisa was a little kid. What did Gayle think she was, eight years old?

"I want to go to the *movie*," she said rebelliously, "And I already said I'd go."

Mr. Canard became really angry.

"Well, you shouldn't have done that before asking us!"

Father and daughter glared at each other.

"It's only a movie," Lisa muttered. Parents could be a real pain.

"It's dating," insisted Mr. Canard.

Lisa slammed down her fork. "You just don't want me to have any fun!"

She stormed out of the room and stamped upstairs, ignoring her father as he yelled after her, "You come right back here and sit down." She flung herself on her bed and burst into angry tears. Downstairs her parents looked despairingly at each other. The generation gap was opening at their feet.

Connie arrived home after her newspaper delivery, deep in thought. There must be some way of attracting Candy's attention that didn't make her look like a nerd.

The house had been pretty quiet since her sister Liz went to college. And now her mom had had to go look after Grandma, who'd had another of her strokes. Mom's sister Louella looked in most days to clean up a little and cook supper for Connie and her dad. This evening the house seemed quieter than ever. Connie listened carefully. "Auntie Lou?"

A voice from the attic called, "Up here."

Auntie Lou was kneeling on the floor, surrounded by cardboard boxes and open trunks, a faraway look on her pretty freckled face. Connie wondered why family junk, which nobody had

14

looked at in a thousand years, was making her look all mushy.

Louella's thoughts came back from the 1960s to Connie's world. She pushed back her pale auburn hair and smiled dreamily at her niece. For a moment she could see herself when she was Connie's age.

"I felt like having a little snoop. Something your mom said about Grandma reminded me I hadn't looked through this stuff in years. Look, our high school yearbook. There's a picture of your mom and me." She slowly flipped the pages, smiling and chuckling. "We were such a team. All the boys wanted to date us."

Connie asked tentatively, "Auntie Lou?"

"Umm..." said her aunt, far away again.

"There's this boy at school...Candy. I don't know how to make him like me. Everything I do turns out wrong."

Of course Louella knew the answer to that. Hadn't she been telling Connie for months? "Well, honey, look at the way you're dressed."

Here we go again, Connie thought. *Why don't you wear a skirt, Connie, and a frilly blouse, Connie. Haven't you any shoes but those sneakers, Connie...*

Louella rummaged in a trunk and brought out a yellow, puff-sleeved dress with a very full skirt. "I looked terrific in this..."

Gross, thought Connie, eyeing it. "I don't know, Auntie Lou."

15

Her aunt was delighted to be in charge of Connie's makeover. Sweeping away Connie's doubts, she delved into trunks and boxes, finding scarves, high-heeled shoes, necklaces. "Trust me, hon." Connie submitted like a lamb to the slaughter. Maybe Auntie Lou was right. She got Uncle Jack, didn't she? And Mom got Dad.

On the way to school the next day Lisa poured out her troubles to Casey. As they waited for Danny, the crossing guard, to escort them across the street, she came to the most difficult part of her problem. "What am I going to tell Griff? I already said I'd go with him."

Casey narrowed her eyes thoughtfully. "You could go anyway . . ."

"But they said I can't!"

"Who says they have to know? Just tell them you're with me."

Lisa was really tempted. She desperately wanted to go on her date, and her parents were being unreasonable, even unfeeling, as if they'd never been young. What if Griff thought she didn't like him? She stepped off the sidewalk, deep in thought. Martin Schlegel's orange and yellow vest whizzed past, his bicycle narrowly missing her in the crossing. Danny looked at her reproachfully. Lisa had never been careless like that.

In the schoolyard Martin parked his bicycle, tucked the vest out of sight and put on a red headband. "Hey, Billy!" he called, "like my headband?"

Billy, in a blue baseball cap, pointed to his head. "No one wears those anymore, Martin. It's baseball caps, now."

"Oh." Martin's heart sank.

Lisa and Casey were still going over their chances of conning Mr. Canard and Gayle. Lisa felt a little guilty about lying to them, but after all, it was their own fault. Anyway, she wasn't planning anything very terrible, just to say she was going shopping with Casey and then changing her mind and going to a movie with a different friend who happened to be a boy. She didn't see why she couldn't get away with it.

". . . and they'd never suspect, because you *never* do stuff like this," Casey was saying. But Lisa wasn't listening; she was staring at Connie Jacobs, who had just appeared in the school corridor.

Astonished onlookers weren't sure whether they were seeing a vision or a nightmare. Connie was wearing a canary-coloured nylon taffeta dress about a quarter of a century out of style. Her hair was upswept and tied with a lemon nylon scarf. Heavy white beads the size of miniature golf balls dangled down her meagre chest. Her wide mouth was almost clownish with scarlet lipstick. On her feet were little

17

white socks and her old blue sneakers.

"Wow!" gasped Casey.

Very self-consciously and with a papery rustle of her taffeta skirt, Connie sat down across the aisle from Candy. After one unbelieving stare he didn't give her a second glance. Even her mom's Giorgio body spray didn't seem to get to him. Something was definitely wrong. Maybe she should have worn panty hose and those awful spike heels that Auntie Lou had made her try on. But they made her feel she was trying to balance on stilts. She dragged her attention back to Mrs. Gonzales's lesson. It wandered again. She wondered whether the itch on her back meant a zit was popping out and whether it showed above the top of this tacky low-backed *thing* Auntie Lou had persuaded her to wear. She wondered whether she should tell Candy she'd done it on a dare.

She tapped his arm. He gave her a "get lost" look and rolled his eyes at Pete and Griff. They all stared at her like she was a bad case of measles.

What to do, what to do...? She followed the boys downstairs at the end of the day. As soon as they were out of class, they all pulled baseball caps from their pockets and put them on. A thought suddenly struck Connie, and she acted without hesitation. Closing in, she grabbed Candy's cap, pushed past him and ran down the corridor.

"Hey, what's the big idea? Hey! Gimme that!" Candy yelled.

"Come and get it! You'll have to catch me!" Connie called back, waving the cap.

He muttered a swear word and took off after her. Candy was chasing Connie at last.

In her excitement she bumped against walls as she rounded corridor corners, her skirt swishing and her beads jumping and swinging. She had no idea what Candy might do when he caught her; she hadn't thought that far ahead. But at least he knew she existed. She pushed open a door, raced across tiles and hid behind another door. Nothing happened. She peeped out, panting and smiling.

Rachel Hewitt was standing in front of a mirror, combing her hair. She watched Connie's reflection. "Hi! What're you doing?"

Connie whispered, "Shh! I'm hiding from Candy."

"Relax, he'll never come in here," advised Rachel.

Connie came slowly out of the cubicle. "But I *want* him to find me."

"In the *girl's washroom?*" asked a surprised Rachel. Connie looked sick and raced for the door. She got there just in time to see Candy disappearing at the end of the corridor.

Connie drooped. Maybe it had been a pretty dumb trick. "I just can't do anything right," she griped to Rachel.

Rachel said, "Why not show him you've got interests in common? You're good at baseball, right?"

Connie nodded. Last summer she'd been the star player on the girls' team. "So?"

"So, Candy plays baseball every Saturday afternoon in the park across from my house. It's a pick-up game. Girls can play too."

It was worth a try, thought Connie as Rachel said goodbye and left. She slapped Candy's cap on her head and stared into the washroom mirror. She had to admit a baseball cap looked pretty silly with a nylon headscarf and a prom dress. "Advice," she told her reflection sadly. "Advice. Everybody's got advice."

She tried not to think about Candy for the next three days. She didn't succeed, but at least she didn't try to attract his attention. After one glowering look he'd ignored her. He was wearing a different cap and she didn't think it wise to bring up the subject. Anyway, his blue cap was in her bureau drawer. If *nothing* ever worked with him, at least she'd have something of his to keep.

On Saturday afternoon, she put on a pair of shorts and a T-shirt and went to the park. A couple of kids were already on the baseball diamond throwing a ball around. She saw Candy arrive and do the bat toss with Billy Martin. She hung back, not too sure how she'd be received. The players had almost all been chosen from the gang of boys and girls hanging around before she made up her mind to go for it. She sauntered over. "Okay if I play?"

Candy looked as if it was anything but okay, but Billy said, "Sure. You can play on our team. We're one man short."

Candy shrugged and went off to join his teammates.

Connie said, "Can't I be on *his* team?"

Billy shook his head. "If you want to play, you have to be on our team."

"Okay," said Connie, "Where do I go?"

"Left field," he told her.

Oh no, not way out there. "That's for kids who can't play," she complained. Billy just looked at her. Connie got the message. "Okay, I'm going, I'm going."

Ten minutes into the game Connie wondered if she was ever going to get into the action. Outfield wasn't exactly the place for high-powered play. Even the shouts of the watching kids seemed a bit thin. She might as well have stayed home. Then the player at bat really connected with a pitch and took off around the diamond. As the ball hit the ground and

21

came rolling into the outfield, Connie chased after it, scooped it up and hurled it to second base. "Out!" yelled the umpire. There were screams of delight from her team and a pleased "Nice throw, Connie" from Billy, but Connie couldn't believe her eyes as a sick-looking Candy Lam shuffled back to the bench. Oh brother, she moaned to herself, won't I *ever* get it right?

Lisa, too, was beginning to wonder whether she'd got it right. When she'd told her stepmother that she and Casey were going shopping at Gerrard Square, Gayle had said she might see them up there. She'd even suggested they all meet for an ice cream! Lisa got out of that one, but when her dad said that baby Nicholas would be with the sitter till six o'clock and they might have time to catch a movie, her heart sank. A movie! What movie? It was all getting to be too much.

"I don't think I should do this after all," she confessed to Casey.

"You *want* to go out with Griff, don't you? Look, if you're so worried, I have an idea."

As soon as Lisa's parents left, the girls went back to the Canards' house. Casey dug out an old trench coat of Gayle's, a Garbo hat and a pair of sunglasses. Dressed up, Lisa looked like somebody playing a part in a 1940s movie.

22

"Are you serious?" she asked. "I can't go out like this."

"You look great," Casey encouraged her. "No one will recognize you."

Well thanks, friend, Lisa thought, as she began to walk up the street, feeling very very silly. Casey gestured to her. "Hurry up! You're gonna be late!"

Griff had arrived at the Gem movie house in good time. It had taken him since right after lunch to get ready. His shirt was clean and his hair combed. He'd even splashed on some of his brother's after-shave. He was really looking forward to this date. If it went well, maybe there'd be more.

At first he didn't recognize the furtive figure who came slinking up, hat well down, coat collar around her ears. "Lisa?" he asked in amazement, staring into the blank darkness of her sunglasses. He felt as if he was making contact with an international spy. "Do you think its gonna rain or something?"

"Never mind. Let's go in," said Lisa.

"There's no rush," he said. "The show doesn't start for ten minutes."

Lisa scanned the sidewalk over the top of her dark glasses. "I don't like it here. Let's go in!"

Okay, if that was the way she wanted it. He bought the tickets. Lisa was still checking the street.

"Someone else coming?" he asked.

"Sure hope not," she replied.

He was a few steps down the aisle before he realized she wasn't with him. He turned back to find her checking out the auditorium. It was getting more like a secret agent thriller every minute. Who was she expecting, the Gestapo?

Griff chose their seats, but Lisa pushed past him and sat further along the row. When a man and woman walked down the aisle, Lisa groaned and slid lower in her seat, almost out of sight.

"What're you doing?" asked Griff. She shushed him.

"You won't be able to see from down there," he whispered.

"Yes I will. I always sit like this."

Weird, thought Griff as the lights dimmed and the music came up. Good thing he really liked her, or else . . .

As soon as it was dark, Lisa sat up a little and peeked over her glasses. Two very familiar adults were sitting a couple of rows in front of them. It was her father and Gayle. She slid way down again. This was terrible. She wished she hadn't come.

Griff was wishing the same.

"Would you take those dark glasses off?" he hissed. "You'll never see anything."

A hand tapped his shoulder from behind. "Young man, would you be quiet? I paid to see this movie."

"So did I," muttered Griff under his breath.

24

He sat in silence for the entire programme. This date was a total disaster! It hardly surprised him when just before the final credits Lisa pushed past him and ran for the foyer. He found her half hidden by a Bogart cutout with her head in a phone booth. She stayed like that until there was no one left in the theatre.

"Too bad you didn't see the end of the movie," said Griff sarcastically.

Lisa tried to explain. "There was someone I didn't want to see — see *me*, I mean." Now that her parents had gone she took off her glasses and hat.

Griff began to get the point. Ashamed to be seen with him, was she? It was like the old days when he was one of the Pirate gang and "nice" kids avoided him. He hadn't thought Lisa Canard would act like that.

"I gotta go," he said. Just as he'd always suspected. Expect something good and it never happens. Lower your guard and — wham! He'd know better in the future.

He started to walk away. "See you later, Lisa."

She looked startled and hurt. "Didn't you like the movie?"

"The *movie* was okay," he said.

"Griff," she said in a very small voice.

He swung around and said bitterly, "You know, if you were too embarrassed to be seen with me, you

25

didn't have to go to the movie." His shoulders were very stiff and his eyes cold. "I never saw you act so weird."

Lisa bit her lip. "Don't you like me?"

He gave her one last look. "I'm not sure anymore."

Unhappy and puzzled, she watched him go. This wasn't how the date was supposed to turn out.

Connie's day hadn't been much better.

Her turn at bat had come at last. Candy was pitcher and she hit as hard as she could, between two infielders. She'd show him, she told herself as she rounded first base to the screams of the crowd.

She slid into second moments before the ball thumped the baseman's glove. Back at the bench her team cheered her. Billy slapped her shoulder. Team supporters shouted, "Way to go, Connie!" Life was pretty good. Then she saw the captain of the opposing team frowning at her. Candy wasn't happy. Connie sighed.

She was back in the outfield. Her team was ahead, eight to seven, the kids shouting "One more out!" as Candy swung his bat. He hit Billy's pitch with tremendous force and the ball sailed way up and out. Candy threw his bat and started down the baseline. As the ball peaked, Connie realized it was coming right towards her. Oh *no*, she thought. Her hero was racing for second base as the ball started to drop. She watched it in horror as she ran, compelled to meet it. From the corner of her eye she could see Candy pounding around the bases. He seemed to be watching her. Billy was yelling, "Catch it, Connie! Catch it!" Candy's team were urging him on. Should she miss it for his sake? It would be so easy. She raised her glove and the ball slapped into it. Her team was jubilant. "Out!!"

Candy looked as if he wanted to kill.

It was like being a star, the way they were all crowding around her and inviting her back next Saturday. But Candy left without a word. She'd spoiled his afternoon — and ruined her own.

Lisa trudged slowly home from the wreckage of her date. She put the trench coat, hat and glasses down in the hall and was going upstairs when her parents called her into the living room. She froze.

"Can we speak to you a moment, please?" her father asked.

She knew it meant trouble. She went in very slowly to face them. They were sitting on the couch, with Nicholas on the rug at their feet. Gayle gestured to a space between them, exchanging a glance with her husband. Lisa tried to cover her discomfort by jingling a toy at Nicholas. They'd seen her this afternoon, she was sure they'd seen her.

Her father said, "Well, Lisa, Gayle and I have talked it over, and we've decided that you *should* be allowed to go to the movies with your friend."

Lisa stared at them in disbelief. Gayle smiled. "After all, you've never let us down." She added in a little rush, "I guess what we're trying to say is we're really sorry it looked like we didn't trust you."

Lisa felt ashamed and near tears. She sat in silence just looking at them.

"Hey, I thought you'd be happy," Gayle said, a little puzzled.

"I'm happy. I'm happy," Lisa said, trying to be. "Really!" She dropped the baby's toy and ran into her bedroom.

Her parents exchanged a look that said, Kids, who knows about kids anymore?

In Connie's kitchen Auntie Lou wanted to know about the game. "We won by one run. I got three hits and made the final out."

"Wonderful!" said Auntie Lou, wondering why Connie looked so tired and unhappy. "And how about Candy?"

"*He* was the final out," said Connie. Her aunt looked sympathetic, but before she could say anything, Connie blurted, "I couldn't drop the ball, Auntie Lou. The team was counting on me. *I* was counting on me!"

She went to her room, telling herself that this was

it. She'd tried everything, and if Candy didn't like her, it was just too bad. She couldn't be different just to please him. She tried to be happy about her decision.

Next Monday morning, still wearing his fluorescent vest, Martin Schlegel was locking up his bicycle. He'd just put on his baseball cap when Billy came by wearing a headband. Martin's face fell. He took off the cap.

"Baseball caps are out, right?"

Billy nodded, studying Martin's vest.

"Hey, I like your vest."

"This?"

"Yeah, nice colour. Where'd you get it? I'd like to get one. Nice colour."

The opportunity was too good to miss. Oh so casually Martin said, "I wear this because it's cool, man, real cool."

In the school hallway Connie, wearing a sweat shirt and jeans, was walking along behind Candy. After a moment's hesitation she hurried to catch up to him, reaching into her bag. She touched him lightly.

"Hey, Candy. Sorry I took this. It was supposed to be sort of a joke."

He took the cap, put it on and smiled at her.

"That's okay. I can take a joke. Sometimes," he

added, in case she got ideas.

They stood, a bit awkwardly.

Connie said, "Well, see you."

They went in their different directions, then Candy hesitated, turned back and said, "That was a great catch you made."

"Thanks," said Connie, holding her breath.

"So you're going to play again next Saturday?"

Cool, Connie, play it cool. "Er— maybe. *Yes.*"

"Great. This time I'll try to get you on my team."

"Okay." Cool, Connie, cool, "Thanks, Candy."

Rachel had a motive when she agreed to have Griff draw her picture. She was posing for him at the stairwell. "Griff," she asked, through her fixed smile, "how'd you like to be art director on our new yearbook?"

"Yearbook?" said Griff.

"Yeah, we're going to have a yearbook to commemorate our last term at Degrassi Elementary School."

As Pete took over the explanation — only because it was difficult for Rachel to explain through a rigid smile, of course — Casey and Lisa came down the stairs. Lisa paused as if she'd like to speak. Her eyes held Griff's for a moment and she gave a shy little smile. Griff turned back to his caricature. "Yeah," he said to Rachel. "Sure. Sounds neat. Glad to help."

Lisa went to the classroom feeling like the day had turned grey. If only she hadn't gone on that date. If only she'd explained to Griff why. If only she hadn't blown it.

If only she'd been herself.

Lisa Gets the Picture

Lisa and Griff wandered past, gazing at each other and sharing a joke. Casey gave them a hostile look . . . .

Lisa Gets the Picture

As their dime dropped into the slot of the school photocopier, Casey and Lisa held hands and crossed their fingers. It didn't help. The machine did its familiar rock and roll and disgorged a picture of what looked like cat vomit. Lisa made a face in imitation of yet another lousy copy of her photograph. Thirty cents wasted.

Her friend tried to cheer her up. "I think it's an improvement, Lisa."

"Well, thanks, Casey," Lisa responded, laughing.

Casey put the original glossy print back on the photocopier. "One more? Maybe if we try it brighter? My treat."

She adjusted the tone, put in ten cents and ran the photograph through again. This time the picture was a lighter mess — left-over breakfast cereal.

"Oh yuck," said Lisa hopelessly.

Maybe using the photocopier to reproduce photos for the Degrassi yearbook wasn't such a good idea after all. It had seemed a brilliant notion after they'd seen that machine downtown work wonders on their T-shirts. But apparently the machine in the Eaton Centre boutique possessed some secret power the Degrassi Elementary School photocopier knew nothing about. That day, the girls were wearing the identical T-shirts they'd had imprinted with a photograph of themselves, cheek to cheek with a big red heart in the background. *That* picture reproduced perfectly. Oh well, back to the drawing board: they had to come up with some way of reproducing photos for the yearbook, and quick.

It was now several weeks since yearbook director Rachel, well aware that Casey and Lisa always did everything together, had appointed them joint class interviewers. But the girls had been so busy with fund-raising projects for the yearbook (a walk-a-thon, a song and dance show, a window washing session) that the down-to-earth business of asking the class members their pet peeves and future ambitions had been swept into the background. And now, with their deadline looming closer and closer, they still had no interviews and no bright ideas about how to get photos into the yearbook. Rachel would not be amused.

Rachel had been beavering away all term, planning, organizing and co-ordinating so relentlessly that there had been more than one mutter about slave drivers and Big Sister. She probably expected the interviews to be half completed by now, and all Lisa and Casey had done so far was interview each other. This hadn't taken long. They already knew all each other's secrets anyway.

There was a yearbook meeting that afternoon after school, and Lisa and Casey had hoped to give their commander-in-chief a reassuring report of their progress. Now it looked as if it might have to be 'fess up time instead.

Lisa said, "We'll have to stick together on this, Casey."

"Okay," Casey agreed. "You got any glue?"

The yearbook committee members were all busy working away when Lisa and Casey arrived on the scene. Judy Erikson's father had given the kids permission to use his garage as the yearbook office while he was away on a selling trip. Mrs. Rothfels of the Degrassi Real Estate office, Casey's mom, had donated an old Underwood typewriter, and Rachel had brought a rickety table from the Hewitt attic. The rather battered chair had been banished from Connie Jacobs's kitchen, and Pete Riley had found the rusty filing cabinet in back of the Wing-a-Way Travel Bureau. He was into negotiations for the purchase of an old copying machine he'd sighted at the same time. Some method of mass-producing the yearbook was badly needed. Photocopying would be way too expensive, and Connie, Rachel's secretary, was no high-speed typist. Her average was about ninety words an hour and her ability to spell seemed to desert her as soon as she sat in front of the keyboard. The yearbook office floor had a deep-pile white carpet, courtesy of Connie, and beside the Underwood was a deep pile of her discarded efforts.

She was pecking away with two fingers when Rachel looked up from her calculations, ready to address the meeting. "Guys, I've got great news. We've finally raised enough money for the yearbook!"

The garage echoed to the committee's cheers. Lisa and Casey hugged each other. Rachel raised a hand for silence. "Now for the bad news. If we want it ready for graduation, we have to finish everything in three weeks."

Three weeks! The cheers turned to groans. Lisa and Casey glanced at each other. They'd never be through the interviews in three weeks. *And* there was the problem of the pictures. Their eyes said it all: Not a word to the director until we've talked it over some more.

First Rachel quizzed Pete about the copying machine. "And don't forget, Pete, no matter how badly we need it, we can't spend more than fifteen dollars." Then she turned to Lisa and Casey.

"How are the class interviews coming along?"

"Oh, fine," Casey said airily.

"And the pictures?"

"No problem, Rachel. Right, Lisa?"

Lisa widened very innocent eyes. "Right, Casey. No problem, Rachel."

Rachel studied them a bit suspiciously. She'd expected at least some excuses and pleadings for time. This was too good to be true. Lisa and Casey met her gaze with guileless expressions. "Trust us!" they said in chorus.

Hmm, thought Rachel, but turned to other matters. She peered over the shoulder of her secretary. No need to ask Connie how the typing was progressing. The floor was answer enough.

It was during Mr. Mackey's talk on careers the next day that Casey got the first glimmer of her big idea. He was reminding the class that once they moved on to junior high school they would have to give a great deal of serious thought to what they wanted to become in the future.

"You're at a very exciting time in your lives, with so many opportunities and choices to be made," he said. Then he asked Pete if he had any plans.

"I'm going to be a mechanic," said Pete with a typical Riley grin. "My mom just had her car fixed. Mechanics make a *lot* of money."

Mr. Mackey smiled slightly. "Money is only one consideration, Pete. It's also very important to choose something you enjoy. Take Griff for example. He likes to draw ..." Casey was suddenly alert. If she'd been a dog, her ears would have pricked up. "...so Griff might be an architect or an artist or a designer," continued Mr. Mackey. "In my case, I enjoyed helping my younger brothers and sisters with their homework, and that's why I chose teaching. Maybe some of you love animals. How about training to be a veterinarian? Rachel here may be a future cabinet minister."

Class laughter and the teacher's voice faded for Casey as she began to work at her idea. She knew she mustn't spring it too suddenly on her friend, who was still very sensitive on the subject of Griff. Ever since that disastrous movie date, when Griff had walked away without a backward glance, he had ignored Lisa. Whenever she tried to speak to him it was as if she didn't exist. Casey knew that, in spite of everything, Lisa thought Griff was a really cute guy and wanted to be friends with him again. If this new idea worked, they could kill two birds with one stone.

That day, as they walked home, Casey casually introduced the subject of careers. By the time they'd reached Lisa's house she'd worked the conversation around to herself. "What I'm going to do is write romances." She made her voice very theatrical as she quoted from one of her future best sellers: "Hand-some Griff looked up. Their eyes met. He could hardly breathe. He trembled at her radiant beauty as she came down the stairs carrying a bouquet…"

At that very moment, Lisa's stepmother, radiant in an old scarf and house-cleaning clothes, came downstairs carrying the vacuum cleaner. The girls broke into giggles.

"What's so funny?" asked Gayle goodnaturedly.

"Oh, nothing," said Lisa through her laughter, giving her stepmother and the vacuum an affectionate squeeze.

"Young lady," said Gayle firmly, "you may go on holding the vacuum. Your room looks like a disaster area. I want you to clean it tonight."

"Oh Gayle," wailed Lisa, "I can't. Casey and me, we've got to work on the yearbook."

Gayle sighed. The yearbook had already been used so often as an excuse for wriggling out of chores that she'd almost expected Lisa to say that. "Well tomorrow then, okay?"

Lisa smiled but made no promises. She led the way upstairs. "We'd better work out some plan for these interviews, whether we do them together or each do some."

Casey looked at the bedroom. Gayle had a point. It seemed worse than usual. Clothes, books and stuffed toys were strewn all over, as if a hurricane had struck. "Wow," she said. "Don't you ever hang up your clothes?"

Lisa picked up a sweater from the floor and dropped it on the bed. "I can never decide what to wear in the morning."

A feeble excuse, but it gave Casey a perfect chance to imitate Mr. Mackey. "That's probably because you're at a very important time in your life, with so many opportunities and choices to be made."

The girls collapsed, laughing. When they stopped, Lisa said, "I wish we had some choices about these yearbook pictures. What are we going to do?"

Casey murmured with a rapturous expression, "He looked up. He could hardly breathe. He trembled at her radiant beauty..."

"Casey, what are you talking about?"

"Griff! We'll get Griff to *draw* the pictures!"

Lisa's heart went bump at the thought of working with Griff. He couldn't ignore her if they were involved in the same project. "That's a *great* idea!"

Casey watched her slyly, an amused glint in her eye. "You can ask him in the morning."

"Me! Why me?" Working together was one thing, but approaching him with the suggestion was quite another. He'd stared right through her so many times already. "I just can't, Casey. Why don't *you* ask him?"

"Because you know him better. And besides, you still really like him, right?"

"Yes," Lisa admitted. "But you know he won't

even *talk* to me ever since that terrible date."

"Look," urged Casey, "what about choices and opportunities, Lisa? Are you going to choose to miss this big opportunity?"

Lisa thought about it. It *was* a real reason to speak to Griff, and they *did* need his help, and he *was* supposed to be the official art director on the yearbook, and it *would* be great if he looked at her the way he used to.

Casey's eyes were twinkling. "Go for it, Lisa."

A slow smile crept over Lisa's face. She gave a quick nod and dissolved into giggles. Casey prodded her and spluttered with laughter.

"Where'd I be without you, Casey?" Lisa gurgled.

"In the soup! C'mon, we gotta decide which kids we're going to interview first tomorrow — after Griff, of course."

Casey was endlessly inventive. She devised a plan for Lisa to meet Griff, accidentally on purpose, by lying in wait for him. The two girls lurked around a corner until Griff appeared at the far end of the school corridor. Casey counted the seconds until she reckoned he should have reached them, then gave Lisa a vigorous push. Lisa stumbled forward, glanced behind with exaggerated annoyance, then showed elaborate surprise at bumping into Griff. She smiled as winningly as she could. "Hi, Griff!

Er — I don't know if you know, but Casey and I are in charge of interviews for the yearbook. We were wondering if . . ."

He'll say no, she was thinking, I just know he'll say no. Griff didn't say no. He didn't say anything. He walked on as if nothing had happened. Lisa stood there feeling foolish. She turned back to Casey. "See? I *told* you he always walks away."

Casey chewed her fingertips in thought. "So, talk to him when he can't walk away."

"But when will I get a chance?" Lisa asked.

Casey didn't know. She fell back on her all-purpose advice: "Wait for your opportunity!"

Opportunity. The word seemed to be coming up everywhere. When they went to Mr. Mackey's class, there it was on the blackboard, along with Money, Interest and Ability, all under the general heading Choosing a Career. A screen was pulled down over the blackboard and a film projector sat in the centre aisle. As soon as the class was seated, Mr. Mackey began. "How do you choose a career? Well, you might begin by thinking about the things you *like* to do. What are your strengths and what are your weaknesses?"

Casey glanced around, sizing up the situation. Here was their opportunity!

"Today we're going to be looking at a film that

deals with just these questions. Watch carefully and we'll talk about it afterwards."

Mr. Mackey called for the lights to be turned off and the blind dropped. He switched on the projector, and the classroom flickered with pale light from the screen. Under cover of the music Casey whispered, "Lisa, Griff can't go anywhere now!"

Lisa gave her a puzzled look. "Well, neither can I!"

Casey nudged her. "Yes you can."

With Mr. Mackey right here? Casey must be crazy. Lisa rolled her eyes with a gimme-a-break expression.

Casey hissed, "Opportunity, Lisa! This is the big one! Go *on*." She leaned across and pulled her from her seat.

Oh brother! Crouched low like someone dodging a crossfire of bullets, Lisa threaded her way among the desks. Some kids stared at her as she sneaked past, but nobody spoke. Telling herself that he'd see her for sure, she managed to bypass Mr. Mackey, get behind the projector and reach Griff's desk. He jumped slightly as she tapped his shoulder, then gave her a hostile frown.

She whispered urgently, anxious to get it over, "Hi, Casey and I were wondering if you would draw caricatures of everyone for the yearbook. We can't afford photographs."

Griff shook his head. "I've got too much work to do. I gotta study."

"Please?"

"I don't want to flunk."

Lisa tried again. At least Griff was talking to her. "*Please*, Griff?"

"No, I've got to pass."

Her voice rose a little. "But you're our only chance!"

He repeated loudly, "I said no!"

The projector whirred to a stop. Mr. Mackey turned around. Griff covered his eyes and groaned. As the light went on, Lisa stood up guiltily.

"What's going on?" demanded Mr. Mackey. He interrupted Lisa's "Uh — er — um" with a stern "I want to see both you and Robin Griffiths after school."

She made another effort. "But, Mr. Mackey, I..."

He said severely, "Go to your seat, Lisa, please. We'll talk about it later."

As she moved away, very very embarrassed, she heard Griff murmur bitterly, "Thanks a lot, Lisa."

She slouched back to her seat, glaring at Casey, who raised her hands helplessly. Mr. Mackey called for the lights to be turned off and restarted the film. Lisa risked a peek at Griff. With his elbow on the desk and his fist pummeling his cheek, he was glowering at her.

46

Nothing had gone right since that awful date, and now things were worse than ever. She'd got Griff a detention as well as getting one herself for the first time ever. She was supposed to help Casey with the interviews after school, and they were still no nearer to getting the pictures. She sniffed hard and blew her nose so that no one, not even Casey, would know that she felt like crying.

At the end of the afternoon Lisa waited nervously as the rest of the class clattered out. She'd seen other kids kept back for detentions but had never asked what it was like. She wondered what they would have to do. She knew that Griff was sitting silently behind her, but she didn't dare turn to look at him. She must make Mr. Mackey believe that it wasn't his fault. It was no use apologizing to Griff. He probably hated her and would never speak to her again.

And then there were those interviews. Casey had told her not to worry, they'd work on them tomorrow, but it was another whole day gone from the three weeks they had left. Oh well, tonight she could stay home and have a great time cleaning up her room.

Mr. Mackey finished rewinding the film and sat on the corner of a desk. "Now. Robin, Lisa. What do you have to say for yourselves?"

Before Griff could answer, Lisa said, "It wasn't

Griff's fault, Mr. Mackey. I spoke to him first. He didn't want to talk to me."

Mr. Mackey looked from one to the other, studying their expressions. Lisa had sounded sincere, and her eyes seemed to be begging to be believed. Robin Griffiths' face was harder to read. He looked both surprised and wary.

Mr. Mackey asked, "Is that right, Robin?"

Griff shot a quick glance at Lisa, then dropped his eyes and nodded. It was impossible to tell what he was thinking.

After a moment's consideration Mr. Mackey said, "Okay, Griff, you can go."

"Yes, Mr. Mackey," Griff replied in a very low voice. He paused for a second at the door to look back as Mr. Mackey motioned Lisa to a chair. Lisa sat down and lowered her head as the teacher began his instructions for her detention. "Lisa, I want you to use your time here wisely. I want you to make a list of things that you're interested in and explain how they might apply to your future. Do you understand?"

She thought she understood, but when it came to writing down the things that interested her she couldn't see what use any of them would be to her future. CLOTHES — wearing them, not selling them. MOVIES — watching them, not making them. GRIFF — no future there. CAMPING IN THE WOODS —

were there any lady lumberjacks? SWIMMING —
how good did you have to be to get medals? GRIFF
— oh, stop thinking about him. ROLLER SKATING
— perhaps she could be a skating waitress and serve
martinis. She began to smile at the idea, saw Mr.
Mackey glance at her and hastily jotted down a few
random words.

She wondered if her teacher wanted to get home
to supper. She wondered what Gayle would cook
for supper. She wondered what Griff liked for
supper — stop it! She wondered what her brother
Noel was having for lunch in Vancouver. She
remembered how Noel used to tease her years ago,
when she and Casey started their Degrassi Street
Journal. Hey, she'd forgotten that she'd wanted to be
a newspaper reporter. She'd start with that. At last
she began to write busily.

Perhaps Mr. Mackey did want his supper. After
about twenty minutes he told her she could go.

"I didn't finish, Mr. Mackey," she ventured.

"You may have until Monday to hand it in. Good
night, Lisa."

"Good night, Mr. Mackey."

The corridor was quiet and empty except for the
janitor who was mopping at the far end. Lisa, her
head bent in thought, started towards the staircase.
A sudden movement as she turned the corner
startled her so much that she dropped her books.

49

"Hi," said Griff. "Hey, sorry about that." He bent down to help her.

"It's — it's okay," said Lisa, her heart thumping. He'd waited! All this time, he had waited!

He said, a bit awkwardly, "Thanks for what you said to Mr. Mackey."

Lisa tried to be cool about it. "That's okay — it wasn't your fault."

There was another small silence, then Griff said diffidently, "Do you really need help with the yearbook?"

Lisa didn't want to push too hard. "There *is* a lot to do," she admitted.

"Because I could help a bit, I guess."

Oh, heavenly Mr. Mackey for giving detentions! She just couldn't stay cool. "That's great!" She tried to clap her hands and the books began to slip again.

"Here, let me take them," Griff offered.

They began to walk down the stairs.

"How'd the detention go?" he asked.

She nearly said, "Detention, the best invention since the wheel," but managed a shrug and an "Okay, I guess."

By the time they reached the main crossing where Danny the crossing guard still stood, waiting for any stray sheep kept late at school, Lisa and Griff were back to being almost as friendly as before their movie date. Lisa would have liked to explain about

50

her weird behaviour that Saturday, but was treating her sudden good luck so carefully she didn't dare take a chance on upsetting Griff. Best to wait. He had asked if she'd go with him tomorrow after school to choose sketching paper and pencils. Maybe she'd explain then.

She could hardly wait to call Casey. As soon as she reached home, she headed for the phone.

"Hi," said Casey, answering after the first ring. "How was your detention?"

"Wonderful!" announced Lisa with a sigh of ecstasy.

"Huh?" said Casey, wondering if she'd heard right.

"Griff waited for me! And he's going to help us with the yearbook pictures!"

"You're kidding! Hey, that's great!"

Lisa bubbled on. "Uh huh, and tomorrow after school we're going together to buy pencils and stuff. It's almost like a date!"

"Hold it," Casey reminded her. "What about the interviews?"

"Oh, let them wait. I'll help you the day after. Oh Casey, this is my big chance. What do you think I should wear?"

With just a faint chill in her voice Casey said, "You'll have to decide, won't you, Lisa? I'm sure you'll think of something."

In spite of her excitement Lisa could tell that her friend was peeved. She suggested, hoping Casey would refuse, "If it's really a problem I can go another time."

"Don't worry," Casey said briefly. She thought, don't worry about promises, Lisa, it's only good old Casey.

Lisa was relieved. "Great. Thanks a lot, Casey. Bye."

"Bye," said Casey, hanging up. And thanks a lot to you too, Lisa. She went back to making lists of questions for the class interviews.

In the yearbook office Connie's slow tap-tap-tap was interrupted by the rattle of wheels outside. The committee could hear Pete giving instructions. "Turn. Over here! All right, this way!" and Karen Gillis protesting, "Slow it down. Slow it down!"

Into the garage came Pete and Karen, wheeling a very old and very used-looking Gestetner 260.

Rachel observed it, less than pleased. "And what's that?"

Pete beamed at her. "Our copying machine. Give me a hand again, Karen. Isn't it a beauty? And it didn't cost a cent! The guy was going to throw it out! Can you believe it?"

"Yes," said Billy Martin. "And I don't blame him."

"Hey," Karen said, annoyed after all the hard work. "It looks pretty good."

"It looks pretty tired." Rachel examined it and swung the handle. It twirled around without resistance, then dangled uselessly like a broken arm. She sniffed contemptuously. "It doesn't look like it works!"

"It doesn't. Not yet," Pete said cheerfully as they all stared at him in disbelief. "But I'll fix it!"

"You!" There was a united chorus.

Pete laid his hand on his heart. "I'm going to become a mechanic, remember?" he told them as if that meant he was totally trustworthy and reliable.

Rachel asked suspiciously, "This was free, right? So you've still got our fifteen dollars?"

"Well . . ." said Pete, "I had to buy some tools and stuff to fix it." He lifted a box from the bottom of the wagon. Not even Rachel's deepening scowl could daunt him. "See, they're really neat! And they only cost twelve dollars!"

Rachel clutched her head. "I knew it! We're doomed!"

Pete wore his never-fear-Pete-Riley's-here expression. "Don't worry, I'll fix it!"

It was too late to make a start that evening, but Pete rushed to the garage right after school the next day. No one else was around. He laid the new wrenches and screwdrivers on the garage floor and selected a couple of tools with all the care of a surgeon. He reached into the body of the machine and adjusted some vital organ. Ha, he told himself, they said I couldn't do it! He swung the handle. There was a noisy crash as nuts and bolts and metal parts tumbled about deep in the Gestetner's insides. Pete's smile of triumph faded. He stood back from the operating table, eyeing the corpse with dismay.

Lisa and Griff were standing in front of a display spinner in the Midoco art supplies store, supposedly choosing exactly the right pencils, sharpener and eraser. But as their hands turned the stand and their eyes looked only at each other, anyone watching could have guessed that they had things other than art supplies on their minds.

Lisa asked, full of admiration, "Are you really going to be an artist?"

Griff said, "Maybe even an architect — if I could just get better at regular school work."

Lisa sighed. "You're lucky. I don't know *what* I'm going to be."

"Don't worry about it," Griff said. "You heard Mr. Mackey. There's lots of time yet."

He smiled encouragingly, and Lisa felt bold enough to broach the delicate subject of their date. "Griff, . . . I'm really sorry about acting so weird that time we went to the movie. My parents said I wasn't

supposed to go and I was really afraid I'd get caught."
She held her breath, waiting for his reaction. It was
all she could have wished for. He began to look as if
someone had just left him a million dollars.

"You should have told me!"

She exclaimed with relief, "I've tried. But you
always walk away!"

He said, a little uncomfortable, "Well, I thought
you'd heard about how I used to be ... in a gang
... and you were kind of ashamed, embarrassed to
be seen with me."

"Oh, I *wasn't*," said Lisa. "I'm not. Really."

Griff looked into her eyes with an expression that
made her tingle. She thought of Casey's romances
and felt her cheeks going pink. She smiled shyly, and
Griff answered her with a slow, warm smile of his
own. For a moment they were the only two people
in the store, in Toronto, in the world. Then, as they
both realized they were getting way out of their
depth, they looked away and made a big show of
choosing pencils.

The next day was a Friday. Usually Casey and Lisa
walked to school together, but that morning Lisa
signalled from her window that she was running late,
so Casey went on alone. At school she decided to go
ahead with the interviews and picked Billy Martin as
a starter. His pet peeve was chain letters.

"And how about your future ambitions?" she

asked, writing *star hockey player* on her note pad before he'd even said it.

Just then Karen came up and stopped to listen. Casey turned to her. "What about you, Karen? Any idea of what your future career will be?"

"I like math and science, Casey. I think I'm going to be an aeronautics engineer."

"How do you spell that?" asked Casey. "And — er — what is it?"

"They make planes and stuff," explained Karen. "It's sort of mechanical."

Behind her Pete shoved a much-thumbed and dog-eared Gestetner manual out of sight and sidled over to greet her like a long-lost cousin. "Karen!"

She looked at him with misgivings. "What do you want?"

"I hear you're interested in aeronautics engineering. Sounds mechanical to me. Me and you, I think we've got a lot in common. How'd you like to be my assistant on fixing the Gestetner? There could be a big future for you in it."

Karen considered it. The last time she'd been Pete's assistant she'd ended up doing most of the work, but this might be kind of interesting. "Okay," she agreed.

Lisa and Griff arrived in the classroom together. Casey whispered to her friend as they sat down. "How'd it go?"

"Great!" murmured Lisa, rolling her eyes and looking dreamy.

Casey giggled. "I bet it was."

"And you know what's even better? I'm helping him with the pictures again today."

Casey's smile faded. "Today? But what about the interviews?"

Lisa waved a dismissive hand. "Oh, we can do them tomorrow," she announced breezily.

Casey put her foot down. "Now look, Lisa, you've got to help. Time's running out. We've got to do some today, and I can't do them all by myself."

"I *will* help," promised Lisa. "But later, okay? Right now I'm helping Griff."

"How?" asked Casey, curling her lip. "You can't draw!"

Lisa became vague and evasive. "I can help. Oh, *c'mon*, Casey. Griff's a *boy!*"

Casey had never seen Lisa look coy before and she decided it didn't suit her. She stared at her with distaste. Romances were all very well in books, but if Lisa's love life was going to become more important than anything else... She would have had a great deal more to say on the subject but for Mr. Mackey's sudden appearance at the classroom door. He was carrying a sheaf of papers for their math quiz that day.

It was lunch time before Casey could give any

more thought to the yearbook. She hurried through the rest of Karen's interview and chose Connie as her next victim. "Pet peeve, Connie?" she asked.

"Earwigs. They're gross."

"Future ambition?"

Connie gave it serious thought while Casey sucked her ballpoint and waited. Baseball player, confectioner, television newscaster? It could be anything except typist.

"I like travelling," said Connie at last. "I think I'll be an astronaut. Or a travel agent. A travel agent for astronauts!"

Lisa and Griff wandered past, gazing at each other and sharing a joke. Casey gave them a hostile look and didn't reply to Lisa's offhand "Hi, Casey."

Connie was reading the interview notepad over Casey's shoulder. "Hey, this looks like fun. If you need any help..."

Casey stared after Lisa and Griff, still deep in conversation. She nodded thoughtfully. "Yeah, I guess I do, Connie."

Lisa and Griff left school together, talking and laughing all the way to Danny's crossing. This was where they would normally have parted, but Lisa was expecting Griff to invite her home or suggest a sundae at the York Cellar. Instead he merely said, "Bye, Lisa." With a cheerful wave to Danny he started away.

"Wait!" she called, very surprised. "I thought we were doing pictures together."

Griff replied, walking backwards away from her, "Sorry. After that math test this morning, boy, have I got a lot of homework to do! I just gotta pass, Lisa, and I'm way behind."

"But..." she began.

He gave a reassuring grin. "Don't worry, I'll do some pictures for you, when I can take a break."

She felt like a burst balloon. "Yeah. Sure," she said. "Bye." She watched Griff go, swinging quite jauntily along the street. He seemed to think homework was more important than being with her.

Danny was looking at her with a puzzled expression. He smiled gently as if he'd like to help but didn't know how. He did the best he could with an encouraging "Have a nice day!"

Lisa gave him a half-hearted smile in return and decided to make the best of a bad job by joining the others at the yearbook office. She could help Casey with those interviews after all.

At the garage the machine doctors were treating the invalid Gestetner. As Karen had suspected, Pete's idea of an assistant was someone to do all the actual work under his supervision. Oily to her elbows, she put a stop to that. "Just hand me the tools, Pete," she requested.

Casey came to her rescue by claiming Pete's attention for an interview. He was torn between the opportunity to talk about himself and the need to instruct Karen.

The conversation went like a rapid-fire routine.

"Screw," Karen demanded.

"Screw," repeated Pete, putting the item into her hand.

"Screwdriver."

"Screwdriver."

Casey interjected, "Pet peeve, Pete?"

"Brussels sprouts."

"Brussels sprouts," repeated Casey to Connie, who was writing down answers.

"No, broccoli," corrected Pete.

"Broccoli."

"Wrench."

"Wrench. No, no, carrots."

"Carrots."

"I don't like zucchini either."

"Pete! Future ambition?"

"Mechanic."

Karen gave him a very eloquent look. Even Rachel glanced up from picking her slow and careful way among the typewriter keys to smile. Karen said, brushing her hair back with an oily hand, "No mechanic would have touched this machine with a barge pole. How come you got it anyway?"

"Because," said Pete, swelling his chest behind his Macho Man sweatshirt, "it was free. And I figured if we could fix it and use it and sell it, we'd make a profit. It's better than renting!"

Hmm, apart from the fixing and using, a swell idea. "Know what?" Karen said, "You're a good businessman."

"Good businessman," said Casey to Connie.

Pete smiled, getting the idea. His Groucho Marx eyebrows wiggled above his glasses like two furry caterpillars.

"Good businessman. *Crummy* mechanic," added Karen, turning back to the copier.

"Crummy mechanic," said Casey to Connie.

Lisa arrived in the midst of their laughter. It all sounded very sociable and folksy in the garage. Just the atmosphere she needed to take away her feelings of rejection. "Hi, guys," she said.

"Hi," they answered. Casey added, "I thought you were helping Griff." She emphasized the word "helping" rather sarcastically.

"He had homework to do," explained Lisa briefly. "So, you want to do the interviews?"

"That's okay, Lisa," Casey said in her most dignified voice. "Connie and I have everything under control."

It was like a dash of cold water when Lisa had expected to be greeted with joy. She looked daggers at poor inoffensive Connie and back at Casey. "I thought *we* were doing the interviews."

"We *were*," said Casey pointedly, "but you were too busy, and Connie offered to help, so . . ."

Coming on top of her earlier disappointment, this was all too much for Lisa. She burst out, "I thought we were friends!"

"We *are* friends," said Casey. "I'm your second-best friend. Next to Griff, of course." She mimicked Lisa's remark of the morning. "He's a *boy*!"

By now everyone was listening and pretending not to. Lisa was very conscious of the tension around her. She knew she shouldn't say it, but it was as if some demon was in charge of her tongue. "You're just jealous!"

"I am not!"

"Yes, you are! *You* don't have a boyfriend."

And I don't want one if it makes me act like you, Casey thought. She said frostily, "Just because you've got a boyfriend, Lisa, doesn't mean you can forget your other friends."

The icier Casey was the more heated Lisa got. "You're just not mature enough to let Griff be my friend too."

Casey immediately became very haughty. She'd show Lisa who was mature. "If you don't mind, Connie and I have work to do." She sailed towards the door, nose in the air. "Come on, Connie."

Feeling very embarrassed, Connie followed. Lisa seethed, tightlipped, then slammed out of the garage. The other three raised their eyebrows, blew out their lips and shrugged.

Lisa stormed home and stamped upstairs, ready to vent her bad temper on her messy bedroom. She flung things about, most of them landing in a growing pile by the door. Out went some old dresses, out went a torn sweater, out, *out*, went her puppets, *out* went her stuffed toys, OUT went the T-shirt with her own and Casey's picture on it.

Gayle, who had heard the stomping footsteps, came to have a look. "Hey, what's all this stuff?"

"Garbage!" said Lisa savagely.

Gayle picked up the T-shirt. "Garbage! You only got this about a week ago."

"I don't want it!"

Gayle had never heard her sound so vicious. She looked on in amazement as a rag doll hurtled into the heap of rejections. "Hey, Lisa, this used to be your favourite."

"I don't need it," snarled Lisa, "I'm almost in junior high."

"Cool it," advised Gayle. "It doesn't mean you have to throw everything away. Some things are worth keeping! Like this."

For the first time Lisa noticed that Gayle had a large album under her arm.

"I was cleaning up and I found my old high school yearbook. Since you're into yearbooks in a big way right now, I thought you'd like to see it."

She sensed that Lisa wasn't ready to be responsive but she went on. "I want to show you my friend Melissa." She flipped over the pages. "We were best friends in high school and twenty years later we're still friends." She smiled at the pictures. "You met Melissa at the wedding. There, that's what she used to look like — and that's me. We've been through a lot together, real friends, a team, just like you and Casey."

You and Casey, you and Casey. The words echoed in Lisa's mind. It was true, they went together like — like Cagney and Lacey or something — a team. They'd been a team. Maybe they still were.

Gayle was saying, "Melissa wrote a great inscription in my yearbook. You should read it." She put the book on the bed and went to answer a ringing phone.

Lisa read the inscription:

Make new friends but keep the old.

One is silver, the other gold.

She stared into space for a full minute, then picked up the T-shirt, folded it and put it in a drawer. A few moments later the puppets and the rag doll were back in their places on the shelf.

*　　　*　　　*

Pete and Karen tried all Saturday afternoon to fix the Gestetner but without success. It was beginning to get dark before they gave up.

"No use," said Pete, admitting defeat. "We've tried everything."

Karen frowned, tugging at her hair in frustration. "I don't get it. It should work now. I wish there was a manual or something."

"Manual?" said Pete. "Yeah, there's a manual."

"Where?" asked Karen dangerously.

Sheepishly, he brought it out of his jeans pocket.

"Now you tell me!" she muttered. Squinting in the darkening garage, she finally took it outside to read in the fading daylight. When she came back, she gave Pete a withering look, then flipped a switch or two on the Gestetner and cranked the handle. The machine lurched into life with all the charm of Frankenstein's monster.

"It works!" exulted Pete.

"No thanks to you, Pete Riley!" she said in disgust.

"It works! We've done it! Say, Karen, let's keep it under wraps till Monday and surprise them. And Karen, thanks."

"No sweat, Mr. Mechanic!"

Monday morning and Lisa hadn't seen Casey all weekend. She'd worked on her room, finished her assignment for Mr. Mackey and thought a lot. She'd decided there was something she had to do and was on her way to the school library when Griff hailed her. "Hey, Lisa. I did some pictures for you on the weekend."

"Great!" she said, admiring the caricatures of Pete and Connie.

"If you want," Griff said, "you can come over tonight and we'll do some more."

She was really tempted. If she said no, would he ever ask again? Well, she'd have to take that chance. "Thanks, but, sorry, I've got to help someone else."

"No problem," Griff replied. "Some other time."

They smiled. Griff went upstairs. Lisa went to the library. She had been right; Casey was there, reading one of her Harlequin romances. Lisa approached quietly, holding her notepad and pen rather tightly. A lot depended on this. She sat beside Casey. "Hi."

"Hi," said Casey, without looking up.

Lisa said, "I'm doing interviews for the yearbook. I wonder if you've got a minute. What's your favourite memory?"

Casey wasn't to be won over easily. "I don't know," she said, shrugging as if it couldn't matter less.

Lisa asked, remembering what she'd written in her assignment, "What about the time we did the

Degrassi Journal and nobody bought it?"

Casey glanced up but almost immediately returned to her reading. "Or when Gayle and my dad had their wedding, and we wore 'jewels' off the hanging lamp? And what about when we had that stupid fight over Rabbit? We almost stopped being friends, remember?"

Casey looked up for longer this time. Lisa laid a hand on her arm. "I'm sorry, Casey. I didn't mean it about you being jealous. I was just sort of mixed up, thinking about the future and stuff and getting excited. Well, I almost forgot we were — are — best friends."

Casey gave a little wriggle. "Well," she said gruffly, "I guess, maybe, I *was* a bit jealous." Her face suddenly crinkled into its familiar merry grin. "Know my pet peeve? Quarrelling with Lisa!"

Pete made a big production number out of the repaired Gestetner. He'd covered it with a sheet, which he whipped off in front of Rachel in a very show biz way.

She took the great unveiling very calmly. "It looks the same as before."

"Show them!" Pete instructed Karen.

He held his breath, just in case Saturday's success had been a fluke.

Karen turned the handle. Bingo! "Ta-da!" she cried with a grand gesture, and the committee broke into cheers.

"Sure is a good thing you're such a great mechanic, Pete," said Rachel.

Was she kidding him? He decided to play it safe. "Actually, it was Karen who fixed it. She's the great mechanic. Me, I'm going to be a businessman."

Lisa and Casey, dressed once again in their identical T-shirts, put Griff's pictures on the machine. Success! And with two weeks left, the yearbook should be ready in time for graduation. Even Connie's typing couldn't take *that* long.

Griff Gets a Hand

Griff looked over to where Lisa was standing alone.
Go for it, he thought.

Griff Gets a Hand

The apartment was in its usual state of disorder. Griff, still only half awake, came yawning into the kitchen to fix himself breakfast. He'd been up very late the night before, battling with his homework, working on the class pictures for the yearbook and trying to finish one rather special one for his friend Danny, the crossing guard.

All the kids were fond of Danny, but to Griff he was someone special — more than just a simple, kindly man who shepherded them across the intersection. In a fit of anger Griff had once called him a "retard," not fully realizing what he was saying. It was then he drew his first picture of Danny and gave it to him by way of apology. The gift marked a turning point in Griff's life. Suddenly his tough-guy days were behind him. Lisa and the rest of the kids began to be his friends; he felt part of a group at last. He could see now that he'd been mad at the world for handing him a crummy deal, and he was glad that the long, empty period when nobody, not even the

Pirate gang, wanted to know him was over. And all thanks to gentle, childlike, trusting Danny.

Of course, Griff was really fond of his older brother Duke too, but Danny would always have his own special place in Griff's affections. He almost wanted to protect Danny, to make sure that his feelings didn't get hurt, that kind of thing. Funny, he sometimes felt as if he were much older than Danny and had to look out for him.

When Danny heard about the yearbook drawings, he begged excitedly, "Will you do one for me too, Griff?"

"Sure," Griff promised. "Right after the yearbook ones are done. A special one for you, Danny — in colour!"

Danny's eyes lit up. "Thanks, Griff! Have a nice day, now."

But somehow Griff hadn't found the time to work on the picture until last night, and it still wasn't quite finished. Now, sitting at the kitchen table, he pushed aside his dish of oat flakes, along with the sugar-encrusted bowl Duke hadn't bothered to put in to soak and a plate of curling pizza from supper the night before. He spread out the picture and began to colour it. But he'd left it too late. Duke called from the bathroom, "Hey, Griff! Time for school."

"In a minute," he shouted back. "I'm trying to finish this picture."

"Griff!" There was a warning note in his brother's voice.

Griff pulled a face. Duke was always beefing at him about getting to school on time. For a guy who had dropped out at the earliest opportunity, Duke sure made waves about his kid brother's education. "You gotta study if you want to get anywhere in the world," he'd say, needle stuck in a well-worn groove.

Griff worked even faster on the picture until Duke, still towelling his head after his shower, looked into the kitchen. "Hey, kiddo, move your tail outta here before I help it out!"

Griff glanced at his brother's bare feet, then sketched a cool-it gesture in the air. "You and whose army?" he grinned before grabbing his bag and heading for the door. Duke shadowboxed at him and went back to the bathroom, laughing.

Meanwhile Danny was busy doing the most important thing in his life, seeing the kids safely across the street. He never tired of blowing his whistle, holding up his bright red stop sign and watching as his charges streamed across the road to school. For all of them he had the same cheery greeting: "Have a good day!"

Billy Martin, Pete Riley and Karen Gillis were crossing together. Billy gave Danny a new slogan button to add to the collection pinned on his sleeve.

Karen gave him a warm smile. Pete had a new joke.

"Hey, Danny, what does King Kong like to eat?"

Danny thought about it. "What?"

"Gorilla-d cheese sandwiches," said Pete. "Get it?" He bent his knees and swung ape-like arms. "*Gorilla-d* cheese sandwiches?"

Danny threw back his head and laughed heartily. That was just the sort of joke he liked.

"That's great! Have a good day, now."

He stood on the sidewalk repeating the joke to himself and chuckling until he saw Griff coming towards him. Then he looked both ways, blew his whistle and crossed the road to meet him.

"Hi, Danny," said Griff, giving his friend a careful look. Yesterday Danny had seemed a bit down and had admitted to having a headache. It wasn't like him to complain, even when the sun was blazing or a snowstorm raged around him, and Griff was concerned.

"Hi, Griff, how are you?"

"I'm fine. How are you? How's the headache?"

"Oh, still there." Danny didn't seem to think it was even worth mentioning. He wanted to talk about something much more important. "You got my drawing?"

"I've got it right here, but it's not finished yet." Griff gave an apologetic smile. "I've been so busy with homework."

74

"You got lots of homework, eh?" Danny asked.

"Yeah," said Griff glumly. "I'll *never* get it finished in time."

Danny searched about in his mind for some way to help his friend. Of course! That very funny joke would cheer up anybody. He began to smile at the thought of it. Griff would get a laugh out of it too; he was sure of it.

"What does King Kong like to eat?"

"I don't know." Griff gave up right away. He knew how much Danny would enjoy telling him the punch line. "What *does* King Kong like to eat?"

Barely able to smother his laughter, Danny announced, "Gorilla-d cheese sandwiches! Get it?"

"What?" queried Griff.

Danny went into the gorilla routine, jumping and scratching. "Gorilla-d cheese sandwiches!"

"Oh." Griff laughed, catching on at last. "Gorilla-d cheese sandwiches! I get it!"

A pair of apes capered across the road, laughing like maniacs.

Griff called back, "I'll bring your picture this afternoon Danny. I *promise!*"

"Don't forget now!"

Griff waved. "I won't. Bye!"

"Bye." Danny's round face glowed. "Have a nice day!"

The moment Griff turned his back, Danny's smile

75

faded. That ache in his head was getting worse. It felt like a bruise behind his eyes. He pushed his cap back and rubbed his forehead. How nice it would be to have someone come along and say "Poor Danny, let me make it better" like they did when he was a little boy. But he knew it was different now. He had responsibilities. It was a shepherd's job to take care of his sheep, not to ask the sheep to worry about the shepherd.

In the school stairwell Lisa and Casey were putting up posters announcing the first-ever grade six graduation dance.

"Are we really going to get to *dance*?" asked Lisa.

Casey said carefully, as if she were speaking to a baby, "That's what the sign says. See, D-A-N..."

"Yeah, funny," said Lisa. "I meant, with boys?"

"No, Lisa," answered Casey, deadpan. "With zebras."

"I've never danced with a boy," confessed Lisa. "I'm not sure I'll go."

Casey couldn't see any problem. "Why not? It'll be lots of fun."

Just then Griff came up the stairs. "Hi, Lisa. Hi, Casey," he called.

"Hi, Griff," answered Casey. "Mrs. Gonzales said to tell you she wants to see you."

Griff looked surprised and a little worried.

"In the teacher's room," Casey added.

He made a grimace. He had a fair idea of what was coming. "Okay, thanks." He started upstairs. Casey called, "You going to the graduation dance?"

Griff looked as though he were thinking it over very carefully. Then he turned to Lisa and asked, as off-handedly as he could, "You going?"

He knew his casual act hadn't been totally successful when Casey started sniggering. But Lisa looked as if she'd been caught totally unawares. "Er — uh — probably," she answered. "I hear it'll be lots of fun."

"Maybe I'll go then," said Griff and went to face what awaited him in the staffroom, leaving the two girls giggling behind him.

Mrs. Gonzales was alone, marking papers. "Come in, Robin," she said. "Sit down." She looked at him kindly but earnestly. "Robin, you haven't handed in your assignments for a long time. Is something wrong?"

He knew the excuse sounded feeble as he said it. "I've been really busy, Mrs. Gonzales, with the yearbook and stuff." He wished he dared admit there were some things he just couldn't grasp. No matter how hard he studied, things he thought he'd learned would slip out of his brain like a fish or something. He had a sudden idea for a caricature of himself, with a head like a fish bowl and little fishy facts leaping out of the murky water.

"Robin?" Mrs. Gonzales seemed to be waiting for him to say something more. There was nothing he could say. She sighed. "Well, it *is* getting rather late. There's only a week or two left. If the work isn't finished, how am I to pass you?"

There was no answer to that. He merely nodded to show he'd heard.

"If there's anything you don't understand or if you need some help, don't be afraid to ask. That's what I'm here for."

Go *on*, say it, he told himself. Admit you're a dimwit who ought to start back in grade three.

"Okay, Robin, that's all, you may go." The opportunity was lost.

He went glumly back to the classroom and sat down at his desk. If only there were someone at home to help with homework. Duke was about as useful as a blunt knife. If only Mom and Dad ...Griff pushed that memory away quickly, as he always did. It still hurt too much.

Oh, well, a few spare minutes to work on the picture. But before he could get started, Pete headed for him with a this'll-kill-ya expression. "Want to hear a joke?" he grinned. "What does King Kong like to eat?"

"Gorilla-d cheese sandwiches," muttered Griff.

"Hey," Pete complained, "that's *my* joke."

Rachel leaned over the desk. "Are you coming to

78

help with the yearbook after school, Griff?"

"I'd like to, honest, but I've got to study."

"Think you're going to pass?"

"I sure hope so," he answered with feeling. It would be humiliating to be the only one in class who didn't graduate. Duke would have *his* say for sure, and for some reason Griff would feel ashamed to have Danny know that he'd failed. Mentally handicapped Danny seemed to want all the kids in his charge to do well.

Griff added a bit of colour to Danny's picture but was distracted by Connie Jacobs's voice behind him. She was thanking Lisa for help with a project. "Hey, Lisa, I got a B-plus! Without your help I probably would've got a C!"

"*You* did the work, Connie," Lisa replied.

"But you helped a lot! Thanks!"

Lisa sounded a bit embarrassed. "It's nothing. You're welcome."

As she passed Griff's desk she smiled, and a most amazing idea popped into his head. Why not? Worth a try. He wouldn't ask here, in front of the rest of the class, but later, at the first opportunity. He started to work on his picture with renewed enthusiasm. Mrs. Gonzales came into the room. He slipped the picture out of sight and opened his history text.

Griff's opportunity came at the end of the afternoon as everyone was leaving. He caught up with

Lisa and Casey. They were deep in girl-talk, giggling, probably discussing the dance or something. He hoped Casey wouldn't hang around to listen. Sometimes she seemed to be having a good laugh at his expense.

"Hi," he said, "Er — hey, Lisa . . ."

Casey got the message as if it had come in on radar. "Bye. I've got to go help with the yearbook. See you later, Lisa."

Griff and Lisa looked at each other.

"So," Lisa asked, "what's up?"

He took the plunge. "Um — I'm sort of having problems with some of the assignments. I was wondering if you could, like, help me?"

"Sure!" said Lisa eagerly. Maybe too eagerly, she thought. She tried to sound casual as she added, "Okay, sure, I don't mind."

Griff felt a little thrill go through him. She'd agreed — just like that! "Really?" he said, glowing. "You mean today? Right now?"

Lisa wanted Griff to think it was by some one-in-a-million chance, so she paused before saying, "Yeah, sure. I've got some free time."

"My place? All *right*! Let's go!"

Griff hoped that Duke, no great housekeeper, had tidied up some. His brother had his own rough idea of housekeeping, but it didn't extend to a whole lot of cleaning and cooking. Griff wondered if he

80

should prepare Lisa by explaining that in the old days Duke had drifted between hotels and rooming houses and had always had someone to clean up after him. But that would mean telling her how Duke had just appeared out of the blue after his parents' accident, while Griff was still numb and confused, had whisked his kid brother away and for the first time in his twenty-four years had rented an apartment and taken a regular job. Griff didn't want to talk about his mom and dad to anyone, not even Lisa. So if the apartment looked like a dog's dinner, tough luck.

His thoughts were interrupted by Lisa asking what assignment he was having trouble with. "Math," he said, "and English . . . and history . . ." She raised her eyebrows. "And geography . . ." Dare he go on? Was that a smile on Lisa's face? "And science. The rest I understand okay!"

Their laughter attracted Danny's attention. He was waiting on the sidewalk. "Hi, Griff! Hi, Lisa! Did you finish my picture yet, Griff?"

Oh, shoot, it *had* slipped his mind, with all that thinking about homework troubles. He hated to disappoint Danny. He said, with real concern, "Oh, Danny, I'm sorry. It's *almost* finished. I'll bring it tomorrow morning for *sure*. I *promise!*"

Danny nodded. "That's nice. Don't forget me, now."

Griff did a thumbs-up and winked. Danny copied him and then went into his King Kong act.

"Bye," he called, "Have a nice day!"

"Bye, Danny," said Griff. "See you tomorrow."

"I thought you already drew his picture," said Lisa as they walked away.

"I did. This one's special though — it's in colour."

When they got to the apartment and opened the door, Griff sighed with relief. He'd seen the place look a lot worse. Though Lisa gazed about with curiosity, she didn't seem surprised or uncomfortable. Duke had left a note to say he was working late and then going for a beer. Griff found hot dogs in the fridge and rolls in the bread box, and Lisa, after calling home to explain she was "helping a friend with some homework," seemed to enjoy helping to prepare supper with him.

While they were eating, Griff cut circles from a sheet of black bristol board. He arranged them on a large blue card he'd marked to represent the universe. "Okay," he said, cardboard discs in one hand, hotdog roll in the other, "First the sun, then — uh — Mercury, then Earth ..."

"Venus," corrected Lisa. "Earth is where you've blobbed the ketchup."

Griff swept the sun, Mercury and Venus off the card, smeared the blob of Earth into oblivion and began again.

Lisa glanced at a framed photograph on the dresser, then studied the laughing couple on the motorbike with more interest. "Are those your parents?"

"Yeah," said Griff curtly.

"Your mom was real pretty," Lisa ventured. There was no reply. "My real mom died when I was two," she continued. "I didn't know her very well. Do you remember what your mom was like?"

Griff said coldly, "Of course I do. It was only two years ago. Anyway, I don't want to talk about that." The taut note in Griff's voice and the frozen lines in his face warned Lisa to drop it. She handed him the cardboard circles.

"Okay," said Griff, setting them out. "First the sun, then Venus..."

"You forgot Mercury."

"You said Venus."

"Yes," explained Lisa patiently, "but Mercury comes first, *then* Venus, then Earth."

"Oh," Griff sighed. At this rate it would take several light years before he got to Pluto, but he'd get it right if he had to work at it till doomsday. He had a mental picture of himself, floating in space, holding a bundle of roadsigns, each with the name of a planet on it. What if he got them wrong and all the little green men on Mars thought they lived on Saturn? At least it would make a good cartoon.

"*Griff*," prompted Lisa. "First the sun . . ."

"Then Mercury, then Venus, then Earth."

They worked on the science project, followed by English and history lessons, until at last Lisa said she had to go home. Feeling much better about his assignments, Griff pushed his books aside for a while and relaxed by finishing the picture of Danny.

The next morning he got up early and studied some more. The sky was overcast and threatening rain, and he had to switch the light on to see clearly. He had his bowl of cereal at his elbow and his head well down over his books when Duke came into the living room, stretching and yawning. "Jeez, you *still* working on that stuff?"

Griff nodded without looking up.

"What's with you these days, Griff?" his brother asked. "All you ever do is study!"

And who was always making a big noise about getting on in the world? Duke must have invented the phrase, "Don't do as I do, do as I say." Griff hunched his shoulders lower. "I have to, Duke. I want to pass!"

Duke shook his head in mild disbelief and went, grinning, to pick up the mail.

"Hey," he said, "an invitation to your graduation!"

Griff looked up at last. "Are you going to come?"

"*Me?*" He couldn't have sounded more incredulous if it had been an invitation to the city jail. "No way you'll catch me inside a school! I had enough of that when I was a kid!" He tipped the cereal box over a bowl and sat down at the table.

Griff said tentatively, eyeing him, "Everyone else's parents will be there."

Duke answered, "We don't have parents anymore."

It sounded too much like a throw-away line. Griff felt himself getting uptight. He looked at the photograph of his mom and dad and tightened his lips into a hard little line. Then he began to throw his books angrily into his schoolbag.

"Something wrong?" Duke asked, glancing up.

"No," said Griff curtly. "I gotta go. See you." He made for the door.

Duke grabbed a bag off the counter. "Hey, Griff, your lunch. And don't let those retarded teachers push you around, eh?"

Griff couldn't help grinning at Duke's remark, even though he'd heard it a million times before. "They're not *retarded*, Duke."

Still, as he clattered down the metal stairs, he had to blink away angry tears. Sometimes Duke could be a real pain. Griff was glad he'd finished Danny's picture at last. He'd much rather think about that than about his brother right now. He knew how happy his friend would be when he gave it to him.

He imagined Danny beaming and saying, "That's great! I knew you'd keep your promise, Griff!"

A light rain was falling. Through the mist Griff saw a familiar orange and yellow figure on the near side of the intersection. He hurried forward, holding out the picture. "Ta-da!" The crossing guard was as surprised as Griff when she turned to face him.

"Where's Danny?" he asked, shocked.

She shook her head. "I don't know. They called me to fill in for him last night. They didn't say why. My name's Thelma."

Griff crossed in silence. Danny had never missed a day before. He hoped his headache hadn't become worse. It was so unusual for Danny to be missing that all the kids had their theories about it. Maybe he'd gone on vacation or been moved to another part of the city. Griff knew neither would have happened without Danny telling him. The most likely thing was that he was sick. Griff decided to find out where he lived so that he could send the picture, like a get well card.

In the classroom, everyone was talking at once as usual, but the chatter quieted as Mrs. Gonzales came into the room. She looked strained and grim, and Griff wondered whether she was frightened of thunderstorms. A distant rumble was rolling through the leaden sky. She faced the class.

"I'm afraid I have some very bad news for you

today. You're going to hear it sooner or later, but I don't like rumours. I'm sorry to tell you that Danny O'Brian, our crossing guard, died last night. He had a stroke."

There was absolute silence as the class took in what she'd said. Then came little intakes of breath and a few stifled sobs. Griff sat like stone, staring at the rain streaming down the windows. The shock of what he'd heard had taken him back two years to that day when a policewoman had put her arm around him and told him that he had to be brave ...and now Danny. It was hard to understand there'd be no more smiling, lovable Danny. No more calls of "Have a nice day!"

Someone's frightened little voice asked, "Mrs. Gonzales, what's a stroke?"

Mrs. Gonzales explained, trying to make it simple. "Well, it's when a blood vessel in the brain gets clogged. The blood can't go through and the brain can't work without blood. So it stops."

Griff stared at the picture, the picture Danny had been so looking forward to. If only he'd finished it sooner, instead of studying. If only he hadn't let Danny down. Typical of life: relax and trust it, and you get hurt all over again. He could feel the old defensive shell creeping around him, the Keep Off signs going up. He couldn't bring himself to join in any of the subdued talk about Danny that went on in quiet moments all day. He ate lunch alone, pretend-ing to study. Even Lisa couldn't get through to him. He heard all the comments around him.

"My grandmother has strokes, but she's still alive."

"Some are worse than others, I guess."

"Poor old Danny, I'm really going to miss him."

"Maybe we should get together and get some flowers or something."

"What about the graduation dance? Would it be right? Now, after..."

"We ought to talk about that..."

What do they really care, he thought. None of them felt like I did about Danny. He sort of *belonged* to me; he needed me, and I let him down.

Lisa lingered in the classroom at the end of the day until she and Griff were the only ones left. He pushed his books into his bag, wishing she wouldn't hover about like that, all eyes and sympathy. His shoulders stiffened at her murmur of "Poor old Danny..." He just didn't want to discuss it. He walked towards the door.

"Do you want me to come and help you again today?" she asked in a hesitant voice.

He shook his head and walked away. When your world is falling to pieces, who wants to study? He knew he'd hurt her feelings by the tone in which she said, "Well, see you tomorrow." But so what, she'd get over it. He'd apologize sometime. He'd never be able to apologize to Danny.

He was sunk in gloom all evening, hardly speaking to Duke when he came back from the laundromat. His brother was full of comical grouches about the machines. "And the dryers *eat* our socks..." But Griff didn't even smile.

"Are you still mad at me about graduation?" asked Duke.

Griff mumbled, "No. Got a headache, that's all."

"Yeah," his brother agreed. "Comes from all that schoolwork. School used to make me sick too!" He laughed at his own joke.

Well *that's* no problem anymore, Griff thought. What's the use of trying? It gets you nowhere in the end. "I'm going to bed," he announced.

In the days that followed, Griff started acting more and more like he used to. He became aloof, inattentive and unresponsive. He contributed his dollar to help buy a wreath for Danny but refused to join in any discussions about the yearbook or the dance and showed no interest in schoolwork. Mrs. Gonzales and Mr. Mackey shook their heads about him time and again in the staffroom. Such a strange boy. He'd seemed to be over the family tragedy, and now... He'd shown such promise, such a waste...

Most of the kids left Griff alone. Let him be like

that, they thought. Lisa was almost the only one who tried to get through the wall he'd built around himself, but he kept ignoring her or refusing to answer.

When she told him that after talking it over carefully, the class had decided to hold the graduation dance after all, Griff stared at her blankly. He'd shown a flicker of interest when she added that the committee was going to dedicate the yearbook to Danny, but almost immediately his eyes became wary and she was shut out again.

One afternoon Mrs. Gonzales made up her mind that she must give Robin Griffiths another pep talk. But first there was a letter to read aloud to the class.

They sat in silence as she read: "Thank you very much for the flowers you sent to our son Danny's funeral last week. We also appreciated all the poems and letters. And we join him in what we know he was wishing — that you all have a happy, happy graduation. Have a good day. Yours sincerely, the O'Brians."

Griff took Danny's picture from his schoolbag and stared at it. He'd sent no letter, no poem. He could have sent the picture, but he couldn't bear to let it go.

Mrs. Gonzales dismissed the class, adding, "Before you go, Robin, I'd like to speak to you."

Rachel stopped by his desk. "Griff, did you hear

we're dedicating the yearbook to Danny? I was wondering—" she glanced down at the picture "—could we use your picture?"

Griff immediately shut it out of sight, inside a book. "No!" he said violently. "It's all I've got left!" He noticed Lisa's reproachful look but stared defiantly at her.

As soon as all the others had gone he went to Mrs. Gonzales's desk. "Sit down, Robin," she said. She looked at him thoughtfully. "You know you haven't handed in any assignments since the last time we spoke. What's bothering you?"

Griff shrugged. No way he could explain it.

She tried again. "Look, I know it's been hard for you, coming to a new school, without your parents. But you've worked hard and you've done well. Don't throw it all away now." No response. She gazed at him unhappily. What can I do, she thought, when he refuses to be helped? She gave him a little gesture of dismissal.

Lisa was waiting at the bottom of the stairs. "Griff," she said, determined to be noticed this time. He gave her a passing glance but kept on walking. She ran a few steps to catch up and walked beside him. There was an awkward silence, broken by Lisa. "How's your science project?" His only answer was a shrug. She persisted. "Do you need any help? I can come over tonight if you want."

He shook his head. "I don't care about school anymore."

She put a hand on his shoulder, forcing him to stand still. He folded his arms like a barrier and stared sullenly at her.

Lisa said softly, "You're not the only one who's sad, you know. We *all* miss Danny."

He was stung into a reply. "Yeah? Well if everyone's so sad, how come they're still having the dance?"

"You heard the letter," she answered. "Maybe Danny would've wanted us to have a dance."

"No way!" He almost spat it at her.

Lisa bit her lip. "He was my friend too!"

Like a river bursting through a dam, Griff shouted, "I'm the one who let him down! *I'm* the one he was counting on! Anyway, *you* don't care about Danny! No one does, except me. So just leave me alone!" He swung away and marched furiously down the corridor.

Lisa was angry too. She called after him, "Sure! Walk away! That's all you ever do!" Holding back tears of frustration she ran in the opposite direction.

Still in a blind fury Griff headed for the intersection, his thoughts churning. Suddenly — there was Danny, holding his sign, nodding and beckoning. Griff broke into a smile of dawning hope. "Danny?"

He rushed towards him. "Danny! Danny, I got your picture! Danny, I got your picture!"

As he reached out to his friend, Danny's face blurred and dissolved in front of him. When the face came into focus again, Griff found himself staring at Thelma. He stopped in his tracks, stricken. Thelma smiled a little uncertainly and escorted him across. All the way up the street he kept turning around to study her. She wondered why.

After supper Griff sat, withdrawn and miserable, staring at Danny's picture, totally absorbed in his own thoughts.

Duke came in from the shower, dressed but still barefoot, a towel around his neck. He peered over Griff's shoulder.

"I thought you had a lot of schoolwork to do. You finished it or something?"

Griff snarled, "Since when do you care what happens at school?"

"Hey," Duke said, taken aback, "I'm your big brother!"

"Big deal," muttered Griff.

"What's the matter with you these days, Griff?" Duke asked, rubbing at his hair. "You're a real jerk, you know that?" He suddenly leaned down and snatched the picture, holding it high out of Griff's reach.

"Gimme that!" Griff leapt up, grabbing at the air.

Duke danced away, lightly as a boxer, waving the picture and taunting him. "Duke, gimme back that picture! If you don't give me back that picture, I'll . . . I'll . . ."

"Yeah? What'll you do? You tell me what's wrong with you and I'll give it back."

In an explosion of rage Griff yelled wildly, "I don't have to tell you anything! What do *you* care? You won't even come to my graduation!"

Duke's face fell, but before he could say anything, Griff snatched at the picture in his hand. Duke jerked away. There was a short, sharp ripping noise and Danny's picture was in two pieces. Griff was stunned for a second, then he gave his brother a violent shove. Duke stumbled backwards onto the couch, knocking the photograph of their parents to the floor with a shattering of glass. Clutching his half of Danny's picture, Griff ran to the door, wrenched it open and stormed down the staircase. He had no idea where he was going — just away, *away.*

He heard Duke calling, "Griff! Griff!" Halfway down the metal steps his brother caught up to him. Though he struggled to get free, Duke held him in a vice-like grip. "Griff, wait —"

"Let go of me!"

Duke said urgently, "Tell me what's wrong, man!"

Breathless, Griff gradually stopped struggling. The worst of his anger had already drained away, but he glared defiantly at his brother. "Danny died. Okay?"

Faintly puzzled, Duke asked, "Danny?" Then it dawned on him. "Oh, your friend the crossing guard? I'm sorry."

Griff said as venomously as he could, "What do *you* care about Danny?"

The brothers stared at each other. In the dusk an orange glow from the neon sign on the bar and grill next door flickered over their faces. The expression in Duke's eyes was hard to read, but his voice was low and his words stumbling. "I care about *you*. You think I don't care about you? You're all the family I've got! If I don't love you, I've got *nothing!*"

Griff suddenly understood that his brother really meant it. Whatever else they'd lost, they still had each other. He felt a choking in his throat, and tears welled up behind his eyes. Childish as it was, he just had to cry. Duke pulled him into his arms and tried in his awkward way to soothe him. "It's okay, boy. Hey, Griff, it's okay!"

Gradually the sobbing stopped, and Griff smeared his wet cheeks with the back of his hand. He gave an apologetic grimace. "Sorry, Duke."

"No sweat," said his brother, punching his chin very gently. "Let's go have a coffee!" He looked down at his feet. "But I guess I better put some shoes on first."

In the grill next door Griff and Duke sat side by side at the counter. Masked by the noise of taped music, babble from the television screen and the hiss of fries hitting hot fat, the brothers began to really talk to each other for the first time since their parents died.

"Tell me about Danny," Duke said, swirling sugar into his coffee.

Griff tried to explain. "We were friends, right? He sort of trusted me, like he wanted me to finish his picture. It was kind of a big thing for him, the picture. But I was always too busy. I let him down, and now he's gone, and he's mad at me..."

Duke shook his head. "People who're dead don't get angry. It's only the ones who're alive who have to worry about stuff like that."

"But," Griff said, "don't laugh, Duke. I see him sometimes."

Duke said quietly but firmly, "All you're seeing's your imagination. Griff, I know. After the crash, I *thought* I saw Mom and Dad..."

Griff looked up from his Coke. Duke nodded. "Yeah, I really did. I missed them, you know. Still do."

They didn't speak for a minute or two, both lost in their own thoughts. Then Griff said, only half in fun, "Don't you go and die on me, Duke!"

"Me? Hey, no way! You're stuck with me for a

while yet!" He grinned. "Better get used to it, eh?"

Griff gave him a wobbly half-smile and sucked loudly at his Coke to cover his embarrassment.

"Er — Griff," Duke said, "I'd like to come to your graduation. If you still want me to."

Griff felt really happy for about one second, before he remembered. "It's no use," he said, sagging back down towards the counter. "I'm gonna flunk anyway."

"Hey," Duke said, gingering him up. "Flunk? How come? Come on, man, learn from my mistakes!"

Duke's encouragement acted like a tonic, and when he added, "Is there anything you can do about it?" the obvious solution dawned on Griff. Time was short, but not too short. Yeah, if she'd agree, there *was* something.

No problem. Lisa was only too happy to agree. She and Griff spent a very studious weekend. On Monday morning, fingers crossed, he handed in every one of his assignments.

There was one more thing he had to do. Without a word he gave Rachel a picture, carefully taped across the middle.

Across the blackboard in the grade six classroom was a banner announcing graduation and the graduation dance. The kids, washed, waxed and polished and nearly unrecognizable in their special occasion outfits, were decorating the room with streamers and balloons. At the back Connie was setting out a buffet with a frosted cake, sandwiches and a punch-bowl. As she carefully arranged plates, beakers and paper napkins, Rachel tapped her on the back.

"Ta-da!" She held out a pile of stapled-together books with brightly coloured covers.

"The yearbook! Fantastic!"

They flipped the first one open to the front page. There was the dedication, "To our friend Danny," and there was Griff's coloured picture of him, holding up his Stop sign and smiling his kindly, never-to-be-forgotten smile.

"I knew we'd do it," said Rachel proudly, "and the Gestetner never let us down once, thanks to Karen."

"And Pete," corrected a spruced-up figure in a business suit.

Lisa, already wearing beads and a bracelet, was pinning a satin rose on her dress. Casey was fixing herself up with over-sized hooped earrings. They studied each other in mutual admiration.

"You're *très magnifique*, darling," said Casey, striking a pose. "And *moi?*"

"*Très jolie! You'll* get asked to dance for sure."

"Do you think Griff'll come?" Casey asked.

Lisa lifted her hands helplessly. "I don't know. I

helped him all weekend, and I *think* he handed his assignments in Monday, but, well, he was way behind. I hope Mrs. Gonzales passed him."

"Maybe he'll come anyway," Casey said.

"Would you?" Lisa asked.

After a moment's reflection Casey shook her head.

The room was filling up with excited kids and their parents. Lisa looked anxiously at the door several times, but there was no sign of Griff.

Mrs. Gonzales, wearing a very stylish jumpsuit, came in the door, carrying the ribbon-tied diplomas. The school principal, elegant in tweed and pearls, was greeted with polite applause.

Mrs. Gonzales mounted the rostrum for her introductory remarks. "It's been a good year all around. I'm proud of all of you and wish you every success in junior high. And now, to present the diplomas to the graduates — our principal."

There was more clapping as she read out the list. One by one the class came forward, received a diploma and joined Mrs. Gonzales on the stage. "...Lisa Canard...Karen Gillis...Pete Riley... Candy Lam...Judy Erikson...Billy Martin..." Not in alphabetical order, thought Lisa, no way of telling whether Griff had passed.

No sooner had Casey come up beside her, than Lisa felt a sharp nudge in the ribs. Griff, in white shirt and tie, had arrived and was hesitating in the doorway. He glanced behind him, stepped back and pulled his reluctant brother forward. Duke too was wearing a white shirt and tie and looked about as comfortable as a mugger at a cop's convention.

The list continued. "...Rachel Hewitt...Martin Schlegel...Robin Griffiths..." No one was more surprised than Griff himself. He went to receive his diploma in a daze.

"Nice work, Robin," murmured Mrs. Gonzales. "I'm proud of you."

At the back of the room Duke was punching the air like a screwball.

A few minutes later Griff, carrying two cups of punch, edged through the crowded classroom to join his brother. "Made it, Duke!"

"Way to go, Griff!" Duke said, slapping him on the back. Griff put the punch down hurriedly. He offered his brother a cup but Duke's eyes had strayed towards Mrs. Gonzales. She was putting on records and trying, without much success, to persuade the boys to join a few brave girls on the dance floor.

"Hey, she really your teacher?" he asked. Griff nodded. "Wow," said Duke, "why didn't they have teachers like that when I was a kid?" He sauntered across the room and with an eager grin asked her to dance.

100

Griff looked over to where Lisa was standing alone. Go for it, he thought. If Duke can shake himself around like a wet dog, without looking like a broomhead, maybe I can too. Anyway, I owe Lisa some thanks. He approached her offhandedly. "Er — want to dance?"

She went a bit pink. "Um — sure."

Casey, dancing with Billy, gave her a told-you-so grin.

Holding each other at arm's length, Griff and Lisa circled the floor in a stately shuffle.

"Thanks for your help," Griff said.

"That's okay," said Lisa. "Glad you made it. And, anyway, *you* did the work." As they passed the bulletin board where the letter from Danny's parents was pinned, Griff said, "I guess you were right when you said Danny'd have wanted us to have the dance. I kinda feel, well, like he's wishing us a nice day."

Over by the buffet Pete had found someone who actually hadn't heard his ancient joke. "*Gorilla'd* cheese sandwiches," he was explaining. "Get it?"

Look for other Degrassi Books

About the Authors

Linda Schuyler, a former public school teacher, and Kit Hood, a writer and former child actor, began their film production company, Playing With Time Inc., in 1976. The company first produced documentaries for use in the classroom, but Schuyler and Hood soon decided that their real interest was in dramatic films. Since that time, they have produced and directed 26 episodes of "The Kids of Degrassi Street," and their company has gained an international reputation for producing high quality, award-winning films for and about children.

Together with Eve Jennings, an established writer of children's books, Hood and Schuyler have combined their talents in these appealing stories to capture effectively the gentle humour and lively adventures of the Degrassi Street characters.

Printed and bound in Canada